INNOCENCE IN EXTREMIS

.

This short novel has been printed in Conjunctions *and in a limited deluxe edition by The Grenfell Press.*

This project is in part supported by grants from the National Endowment for the Arts in Washington, D. C., a Federal Agency, and from the Rhode Island State Council on the Arts.

Library of Congress Cataloging in Publication Data
Hawkes, John, 1925—
    Innocence in extremis.
    I. Title.
PS3558.A82I46 1985   813'.54   84-29232
ISBN 0-930901-29-0
ISBN 0-930901-30-4 (pbk.)

INNOCENCE IN EXTREMIS

John Hawkes

Burning Deck
Providence

In the summer of 1892, when Uncle Jake had barely attained the age of twelve, his father determined that the time had come to return with his proud family to France. His household was then exemplary of the Deauville spirit, including as it did three young sons and their infant brother, a female secretary, five maids, an indomitable and handsome wife who in her Irish pride countenanced his carnal relations with maids and secretary without a word of objection. His sons, excluding the infant, were already taller than their mother and unmistakably of the male Deauville line, though the oldest was but fourteen and the youngest ten. They were large, his sons, big-boned and masculine, though they were only boys. The infant, to whom the father paid scant attention, proclaimed in the features of his tiny face that he too was a Deauville.

Of the women in the father's employ, the secretary was his favorite, with her firm body, lewd mind and auburn hair, which was the source of Uncle Jake's later interest in women with red hair, while three of the maids were hardly older than his three older sons yet totally adaptive to his impulsive ways. Two of the maids were among those he had originally brought from France, and the qualities that accounted for their survival earned the secretary's envy and his own highest personal esteem. They were special women, who could survive so long in his affection and satisfy for such a length of time his needs. The youngest maid had the palest blonde hair he had ever seen; the oldest, who was one of the two French maids, had robust small breasts that made him think of the eyes of an owl. The maids, from first to last, were easily amused, pretty, and created day by day the gossip of which they were themselves the subjects and on which they thrived. They hid their ankles, one and all, and wore black uniforms, white aprons, and small white hats. They worked obediently and deferentially for the Irish matriarch who, at the age of forty, swept through the rooms and halls of Deauville Farms with a grace and grandeur that constantly aroused his admiration and now and again his desire. The secretary was an excellent rider, as was his wife, though the Irish matriarch had for years refused to join his day-long outings on horseback. His boys were provided with shaggy, honey-colored

ponies. If he could have stood them all in a row—
sons, maids, secretary, wife—they would have shone,
each one of them, male and female, large and small,
with the vigor he single-handedly inspired.

The ten members of his household, plus the
infant, were all he wanted—except for his horses, his
stables, and the occasional strange face and figure
to lend spice to the sauce, as he thought of it. In the
summer of 1892 he considered himself nothing if
not the head of the household. He was forty-four
years old, athletic, aristocratic, a heavy-set six-footer
who sat his horse like a Burgundian baron and
enjoyed the flesh of his maids and was admired by
his male friends as the worthiest womanizer of them
all. He was a sexual despot and, he knew, would
never be more handsome. He was his father's ninth
and youngest son, his father's favorite, the only son
the Old Gentleman had intended consciously to
sire. Now he was the man his father had wanted him
to be. Now was the time to return to France, to
transport his entire family across the seas for a
protracted stay in the chateau near Chantilly. He
wanted to present his family to the Old Gentleman.
He wanted to witness the Old Gentleman's pleasure
and receive in person his approval. He wanted to
arrive in the fall, despite the risk of a rough crossing,
in time for the grape harvest and the fox hunting
season.

He wrote a simple letter to his father in his florid

script. He booked their passage. He ordered them to
haul the luggage up from the cellars, down from the
attic. He supervised the packing of the new ward-
robes he had provided for each and every member
of his household, including the maids. The boys and
secretary must take their riding clothes and leather
boots; the maids packed up the household linen, sat
on the trunks so that he might strap down the lids.

His proud wife was disinclined to make the voyage, since she did not want her husband's infidelities
and her own conjugal martyrdom exposed to his
parents. But she said nothing about her disinclina-
tions and through their weeks of preparations carried
herself with a haggard dignity that lent a semblance
of maturity to the scurrying of the little maids. It
was the first time in their married lives that her
husband had intruded upon her matriarchy, inter-
fering in matters that were rightly hers, since though
the maids were his for pleasure still the work they
did was at her own strict and magisterial bidding.
(The secretary, who ostensibly helped him with the
affairs of the stables, generally kept to her rooms in
a separate wing that he had added to the house for
her.) But once her husband had fixed his mind on
his father, and could use the excuse of family pride
to bundle them all off to France for a filial visit to
Chantilly, then she was helpless to do anything other
than tie up her fine black hair in a dusting scarf, as if
she herself were one of the maids, and submit to
his plans.

The preparations lasted for six weeks. It was a period of the keenest anticipation for Uncle Jake, a time when his sense of well-being equaled in its way the bountiful sensations that had come so suddenly and unexpectedly upon his father. Until then Uncle Jake's boyhood had been tranquil, secure, in a way sensual even though the maids refrained from making the slightest gesture to disturb the innocence of himself and the two brothers with whom he spent most of his time, no matter how erotically well-tuned they had become, those pretty maids, thanks to the father. Nonetheless by then Uncle Jake was living on deep-dish blueberry pies spread thickly with the richest cream still warm from the cow, and liked nothing better than lying in his narrow bed up under the eaves and listening to the falling rain while eating an entire box of chocolates slowly, piece by piece. The cook, a kind woman not much older than the two French maids, took special pains to satisfy his boyish appetite for sweetness; the old gardener instilled in him a love for flowers; with his brothers Granny and Doc he spent endless mornings leaving drops of tender blood on the tips of thorns while gathering great buckets of berries for his pies. He and Granny and Doc were shy, well-mannered boys who helped the gardener, watched the cook put up preserves in her immense, slate-colored kitchen under the keen eye of their mother and who strolled hand-in-hand about the shady or sunny acres of Deauville Farms.

Dutifully the three boys exercised their ponies; their riding master praised them to the father as diligent and responsive young horsemen. But surrounded as they were by stables, stallions, brood mares, shiny foals, clever stable boys culled from the lower classes, and owning as each of them did his own pony, nonetheless they did not share their father's equestrian obsessions and quietly kept to themselves, preferring their mother to their father, the cook and maids to the stable boys, and the gardener to the riding master with his little sharp spike of a moustache and long whip. Yet the world of their father's stables offered them the source of their only prank, since among the blooded animals was one, an ungainly blue-black beast which the father for sentimental reasons did not have shot, though it was old and broken, and it was this creature and not the ponies that engaged the interests of Uncle Jake and Doc and Granny, and turned them into pranksters. Once a month they stole the blue-black horse. Without saddle, without bridle, with nothing to guide the old horse but a short length of rope tied to its halter, in this way they climbed on its back, all three of them, and raced in gleeful circles around a distant and tree-screened field, Granny in front and tugging on the rope, Doc in the middle and clinging to Granny's waist, and Uncle Jake sitting backwards and beating upon the old horse's bony rump with a heavy and resounding stick. In no other way were they fractious; only mounted on the ancient blue-black horse could they enjoy their father's world and rebel against it. The riding master knew of their mistreatment of the horse but kept their secret.

Thus Uncle Jake was a mild boy, except when beating the horse, an attractive twelve-year-old encouraged to spoon the thick warm cream onto his pie with a ladle, and his mother's favorite. Then into his already privileged existence there came the prospect of a trip to France. Uncle Jake and Granny and Doc became as excited as the five maids over the promise of ship and Eiffel Tower and all the unknown delights of a foreign land. Naturally the two French maids were happiest of all, and among the three older brothers it was Uncle Jake who most enjoyed their red-eyed pleasure and the spontaneous way they hugged each other, and himself as well if he were near at hand, whenever they thought of their good fortune. France was the only place for them, despite their attachment to Monsieur Deauville, as they called him, and now, for the first time since their arrival in America, they were going back. So Uncle Jake followed them about or watched his father strapping down the lids of the trunks or carried the infant Billy Boy in his arms and attended on his mother's proud bustling.

For six weeks the entire household was in disarray, with closets and cellars and attics emptied and

trunks and valises and hat boxes piled in all the
hallways and in all the rooms, and Uncle Jake, who
had never thought to question the stability of his
mother's matriarchy, which was as pure and perman-
ent as the solemn tinkling of the polished old music
box she kept in her room, now found himself
delighted by the havoc wreaked on their tranquility
by his father. And suddenly his father, rarely seen
about the house, was everywhere, and no longer did
he smile down at Uncle Jake in his distracted fashion
as he did whenever he happened to notice his second
son which was not often, but now tousled his hair,
caught him playfully by an arm, and spoke to him,
however briefly, about the ship and the Eiffel Tower
and the chateau near Chantilly. Now when Uncle
Jake drew close to watch his father kneeling beside
one of the trunks that would take three men to
carry, as his father said, and saw his father reach
up and tweak the thin ankle of one of the young
maids seated atop the trunk, now Uncle Jake enjoyed
his father's gesture as much as the maid and happily
joined in their laughter.

It was a smooth crossing, especially for so late
in September. Furthermore, the head of the family
had booked their accommodations with discretion, so
that his wife's stateroom and his own had a connect-

ing door and adjoined the stateroom assigned to the three boys, while the secretary was placed at the other end of the upper deck in a stateroom adjacent to that of the two French maids. The other maids were consigned to a single cabin below decks. These arrangements were pleasing to everyone concerned since the connecting door between husband and wife was locked each night by the Irish matriarch, allowing her husband freedom to host at will the secretary or one of the French maids, which in turn so conveniently allayed the needs of the head of the family that for the entire trip he flatly and happily denied himself the three younger maids. For their part the younger maids were so exhilarated merely at finding themselves aboard a ship that they missed not a jot the sexual attentions of the master and found the snug cabin below decks grander than the staterooms up above. Even the seating plan for their meals contributed, like weather and staterooms, to the delights of the long crossing. The parents and three boys were grouped together at the Captain's table, so that the handsome matriarch was spared the indignity of having to eat elbow to elbow with the secretary; the secretary and the two French maids ate together in the second seating, and all the agreeable circumstances of the voyage and the very fact of sailing on a French ship toward their native France raised in the maids such a childish bloom of affection and well-being that they quite overcame the secretary's envy. The younger maids were served in the third seating with the rest of the servants which was exactly where they were most at home.

Clear skies, flat seas, rightness prevailing throughout their entire shipboard situation, and games shared by father, sons, maids and secretary on the white deck under the benevolent supervision of the matriarch in her deck chair — here was a family accord hitherto unknown to Uncle Jake, despite chocolates and blueberry pies and the love of his imposing mother at Deauville Farms. Now Uncle Jake strode the deck with Billy Boy in his arms and heard his family admiringly discussed by the passengers and heard himself identified as one of its members. His father laughed throughout the voyage, his mother smiled. Never had he known such contentment as when at the rail he cradled Billy Boy and raised the tiny bonneted head for a kiss or, shading his eyes, scanned the horizon for the coast of France.

They arrived at Le Havre on the last day of September and only a day or so ahead of the first storm of the season. The entire entourage assembled for the landfall. The air was crisp, French ships and French docks and derricks lay all about them in a bright sunlight that had shone on kings. The French maids cried, the proud and lascivious secretary joined

them without intending to, and the head of the
household stood speechless at the sight of the France
of his birth. There in the midst of her family the
matriarch gathered herself to her full height at the
rail and in a profusion of baby blankets and a shawl
of Irish wool gave suck to Billy Boy as if to gird
herself in motherhood against that nation of decadence which she saw clearly enough in the harbor
and city sprawling near and far in the autumn dawn.
She faced as best she could the distant array of tri-
colored flags, the plains of gold. Beside her stood
her favorite son who now and then reached over and
drew the shawl and blanket more protectively about
his mother and Billy Boy, a baby blissfully nursing
with all of France at his back. And next to Uncle
Jake stood Granny holding by the hand the ten-
year-old Doc. They were dressed in caps and jackets
and long trousers, and only Granny, at fourteen,
was conscious of the secretary and giggling maids
surrounding his father. But he too stared ashore with
the eyes of innocence.

For ten days the family remained in Paris where
the crisp clear weather returned on the heels of the
first storm of the season. The father accompanied his
sons and the young maids to the middle platform of
the Eiffel Tower, at that time in its majestic infancy

and the newest wonder of the world. It rose like an
unclothed iron marvel to an astounding height and
then and there, with its panorama of spires and
chimney pots spread out below, implanted in Uncle
Jake his future fear of heights, though on that windy
platform Granny held him around the waist and Doc
clutched his arm. All three boys much preferred the
pond in the famous gardens to the Eiffel Tower,
when the two French maids proudly took their
charges to see the last of the toy sailboats of the
year. Similarly, the young American maids were far
happier returning the glances of every Frenchman
they passed on the boulevards than they had been
on the middle platform of the famous Tower. The
red-headed secretary and the head of the household
were equally stimulated by the sight of sweating
girls flouncing in a raucous line with their skirts held
high — a sight the secretary and French-American
Deauville shared every night of their stay. For her
part, the Irish matriarch insisted that she be left
alone in her hotel room with Billy Boy and vases of
fresh roses that appeared mysteriously each morning.

At last and in another flurry of activity the
family gathered before the small but elegant hotel
and took their places in carriages provided by the
Old Gentleman — there were three carriages for the
family and two for luggage — and sped off toward
Chantilly.

The approach to his grandfather's chateau was through a wood so carefully tended that it resembled a park and through a village of small and colorful shops and houses as old as the Deauville chateau itself. Beyond the village, across a rolling expanse of green fields that looked as carefully tended as the nearly artificial forest, lay the chateau. On the morning that was the last of the journey Uncle Jake was seated beside his mother in the first of the five carriages. Never had he been so alert to his own perceptions and was highly amused when from the carriage window he saw that men with long brooms of bound tree branches were sweeping the floor of the forest. He was grateful for the luxurious interior of the carriage, upholstered as it was in black leather as smooth as satin, and for the contented and expectant expression on the face of his father who, with arms folded and flanked by Doc and Granny, sat facing himself and his mother who was of course still cradling in her arms his swathed and sleeping infant brother.

When the five carriages started across the frosted fields, and Uncle Jake saw on the far edge of the fields the Deauville chateau like a jewel box in a sea of green, he pressed his face to the carriage

window and in the instant acquired that pride in his
family name that would last a lifetime.

Horns sounded. The dappled gray horses, lathered
in harness and plumed in frosted breath, slowed to a
trot. The string of five carriages passed through the
gardens and sculptured hedges that fronted the
chateau and, in a grand clatter, entered through the
high wrought iron gates into the courtyard of the
Old Gentleman's chateau. The five carriages came to
a halt. The twenty horses snorted. The music of
arrival rang out from the shod hooves and ancient
cobblestones. The sunlight of early autumn shone
down upon the crescent of carriages and all those
ranged as in military ranks to greet them. The
journey had ended and the American Deauvilles
alighted into the festive grandeur of the French
Deauvilles.

For a moment no one moved in the silence. Shyness
suffused the pleasure of the Americans, though the
Irish matriarch stood boldly forward with the sleeping Billy Boy, whom she had nursed in the carriage,
once again dozing in her arms. Wide smiles strained
the faces of the French Deauvilles who stood stock
still except for the maids and scullery maids who
were already tensed for curtsying and the male
servants who were unconsciously twisting their caps
in their hands. The hats of the French ladies, filmier
and wider of brim than any such hats Uncle Jake
had ever seen, floated and fluttered among the
French Deauvilles like regal swans.

Then the Old Gentleman stepped forward, his ninth son stepped forward, the two embraced, in French fashion kissed each other twice on both cheeks.

Then relief, confusion, a breaking of ranks. Horses and carriages were driven out of the courtyard; exclamations in French and English filled the air; Uncle Jake and Granny and Doc stayed close to their mother in the milling crowd. Somehow the old Gentleman was able to reform his household into a single receiving line that stretched halfway around the ivory-colored walls of the courtyard. He, his wife and a woman quite mysterious to Uncle Jake were last in that line and the youngest scullery maid was first. Uncle Jake's father, all at once as gracious and European as the old patrician himself, organized his little group into a similar order and led them down the full length of the receiving line, nodding to the French servants, who curtsied or hung their heads according to gender, and presented his wife and sons to his father, his mother, his brothers, and to the mysterious woman. The young American maids were not adept at curtsying and charmed everyone with their efforts; the two briefly repatriated French maids, wiping their wet cheeks and rubbing their red eyes, were allowed to kiss the hands of the Old Gentleman, his wife, his eight sons, and the mysterious woman. The youngest American maid, she whose hair under its white cap was so fine and blonde as to suggest the palest light tinted with the

brightest silver, floundered prettily at the feet of the
Old Gentleman in a way that amused them all and
prompted in the old patrician a hint of surprise and
appreciation that went unnoticed except by Uncle
Jake and his father and his father's secretary and the
little maid herself. As for the secretary, his father
presented her as swiftly and unobtrusively as he
could and thoroughly concealed his secret pleasure at
observing, as only he and Uncle Jake observed — and
of course Uncle Jake saw only signs and not their
import — that the Old Gentleman was even more
smitten by the red-headed woman, in whom brazen-
ness was a kind of grace, than he had been by the
youngest maid.

When it came his turn to bow to the mysterious
woman, Uncle Jake found himself singled out from
his brothers. He felt his father's hand on his
shoulder, he saw Granny escaping from the mysterious woman as fast as he could and knew that she
had hardly deigned to recognize poor Granny, just
as in the next moment she would dismiss the suddenly foolish Doc. And he now was next in line.
She was small, quite as small as the smallest of the
American maids, and yet she was more quietly
imperious than any woman in the courtyard, including both his mother and grandmother, whose size
alone should have made them superior to the mysterious woman but did not. Despite her small size, or
perhaps because of it, her shape was in itself a

flaunting of her spirit, a fulfilling of the female form
unattained even by his mother and grandmother.

His father pronounced his name, stepped back, for
an instant left him face to face with the mysterious
woman. He was embarrassed to find himself taller
than she; he was embarrassed to be standing still in
the line; he was embarrassed to be so obviously and
unaccountably the object of her attention. And to
him this woman was in herself embarrassing: in her
steady eyes, in the glossy pearls that lay on the
green bosom, and most of all in the small and
narrow face which belonged in a locket. Her face
was as hard and glossy as the pearls she wore; it
was youthful yet streaked with age. Before that little
face he blanched, just as the mysterious woman
extended her hand, which she had not done for
Granny, and what could have been worse than that
proferred hand in its tight black calfskin glove? Was
he to shake the mysterious woman's hand or kiss it?
He did not know. He quivered, wiped his own hand
on his trousers. But then the mysterious woman
resolved his dilemma and mortified him both at
once. Before he could move she raised her hand
still higher and reached up and with her tiny fingers
brushed back his hair and stroked the curve of his
ear. Large ears were characteristic of the Deauville
males, and even then Uncle Jake's ears were large.
He was as self-conscious of his ears as to his height.
And the mysterious woman had stroked his ear with

the tips of her fingers. He had no idea who she was
or why she was there in the courtyard. He did not
understand why his father had not said her name
yet knew her well. He did not understand what she
had meant to do or why or by what right. But she
had touched him — and most visibly.

Then it ended. His father laughed, and there was
his grandmother, whom he had waited all these
weeks to meet, and just beyond her the Old Gentleman. Again the courtyard was filled with the sounds
of French, the sounds of English, and in the embrace
of his grandmother, who was taller and more sub-
stantial even than his own mother, Uncle Jake recovered at once his innocence and enthusiasm for
France. He gave himself up completely to his grandmother's embrace.

At twelve Uncle Jake was unable to formulate
what were in fact his feelings for the past and what
was to become in later years his obsession with
genealogy. Nonetheless, for that moment in his
grandmother's arms he knew the vague sensations of
reaching back to the beginnings of his father's life.
His grandmother's sheer bulk and beauty, about
which there could be no question, seemed to justify
still further the trust he had so recently begun to
place in his father. He had found himself liking his
father before leaving Deauville Farms, and now he
liked his grandmother still more. To be hugged by
this large woman dressed in gray was to confirm

his own place in the family line, to convince him that he too was wanted as a Deauville heir. She was strong, warm, and more than his mother, smelled like a person who spent her life giving birth to boys. But little did he know that she had borne her first son at the age of sixteen and detested all males young or old and thought him nothing but disagreeable even as she took him, as he thought, to her heart.

Then up rose his grandfather like a stone figure torn from a tomb. Since August Uncle Jake had wanted to meet his grandmother, but since August he had merely worried about meeting his grandfather. Now could the oldest living male Deauville be anything but frightening to a boy like himself? And if the grandfather resembled not the father whom Uncle Jake was coming to trust but the father who, since Uncle Jake's earliest days, had made his second son uneasy at best, defensively indifferent at worst, what then? Might not the grandfather destroy in the instant all the good of the grandmother?

Uncle Jake peered up in total vulnerability at his grandfather; the bewhiskered old patrician stood straight as a tree and, bejeweled and formally attired as he was, could not have been more intimidating to his grandson. And whereas Uncle Jake had just happily discovered in his grandmother his father's beginnings, now, for the instant, he saw in his grandfather his father's more recent years. The Old Gentleman's

size, bearing, and facial features, behind the whiskers,
were those of Uncle Jake's own father; Uncle Jake
might have been staring at his own father cloaked in
advanced old age. In his grandfather's face he saw
the familiar features — the sensuous lips, the imperious nose, the lordly forehead — and that same
expression of some inner secret life which Uncle
Jake had seen so often and to his extreme discomfort
on the face of his father. But the worst of it was
that in the old patrician's visage Uncle Jake caught
hints not only of his father but of someone even
more perplexing. The old patrician reminded Uncle
Jake not only of his father but, more dreadfully, of
the mysterious woman. From the aged eyes and the
translucent facial skin there shone forth the selfsame
quality of youth that also distinguished the face of
the mysterious woman. It was a quality of youth that
scarred and made compelling the faces of the old
patrician and the mysterious woman. It stirred the
ripples of Uncle Jake's perceptions into a terrible
turbulence: he now intuited that his grandfather and
the mysterious woman were far more advanced in
whatever it was that he most feared in his father,
and Uncle Jake was so shocked at what he now
knew unconsciously, as the Old Gentleman was happily and consciously intrigued by what he had seen
in his grandsons, and especially in Uncle Jake —
namely, an innocence that it had never occurred to
him could exist in a male.

Uncle Jake was never a mentally proficient boy or man, as no Deauville ever was, but he possessed a naive sensibility and so, confronted now by his grandfather, he was overwhelmed by discomfort. But now it was the Old Gentleman himself who put Uncle Jake once more at his ease. The Old Gentleman inclined his head and smiled down at Uncle Jake as if at some greatly pleasing rarity of nature — a dove the color of cobalt blue, a monarch butterfly with four pairs of wings — and bowed to his young grandson with unrestrained cordiality. His smile was agreeable, his breath smelled of feasts and forests, his bow was so simply and sincerely executed that Uncle Jake was able to return it in like manner and without blushing, though he had not until this moment bowed to anyone, man or woman, in his life. Furthermore, the Old Gentleman not only bowed to Uncle Jake but then, after the boy had bowed in his turn, seized Uncle Jake's soft hand and shook it and placed his other hand on the young boy's manly shoulder and squeezed it, as Uncle Jake's own father had recently begun to do.

In the hubbub and after giving Uncle Jake his benediction, so to speak, while greeting Granny and poor Doc with unfair perfunctoriness, the Old Gentleman, who was known for his distaste for children in general and infants in particular, suddenly took it into his head to bestow upon the youngest American Deauville an honor that would mark the infant's future as brilliantly and permanently as would a golden rose tattooed on his little chest. The Old Gentleman meant, that is, to hold his youngest grandson in his arms, a gesture which the Old Gentleman had never been known to make in all his days as a patrician, having refused to hold on his lap or so much as touch even the infant males whom he himself had fathered or to allow at his table any person, including his own nine sons, who had not yet attained majority.

Now, himself surprised at his sudden generosity and so all the more pleased by it, the old patrician turned again to his handsome daughter-in-law and magnanimously and unmistakably reached for the child she was proudly holding against her breast. Only those standing closest to the Old Gentleman and the Irish matriarch saw what was happening and began to smile. At the same time and for no reason whatsoever a hush fell over the courtyard, and it was in this gratuitous silence that an incident devastating to Uncle Jake was fated to occur. The silence alone made him timorous. But he was standing close to his mother, like a shy acolyte, and could not help but appreciate, though anxiously, his mother's pride as the old and smiling patrician faced her suddenly with his arms wide and his forehead mottled in happiness.

"May I?" asked the Old Gentleman and looked upon his daughter-in-law as if she had long been his favorite instead of a woman whose very strangeness had helped to whet his appetites and whose child would securely serve as a plump little bridge between himself and the handsome mother.

The Irish matriarch inclined her head and, quite preserving her dignity, smiled unsuspectingly at the old patrician, curtsied gracefully and almost imperceptibly, and stepped still closer to the oddly stimulating personage of her father-in-law. She appreciated his kind regard and grandfatherly concern for her child; she saw to it that together she and the old patrician affected a slow and careful transfer of the infant. They overcame the slight awkwardness of entangled arms and close bodies; together they managed the transfer without a slip. She saw her child settled stiffly against the old patrician's chest, and with unaccustomed and thoroughly concealed eagerness she fussed to rearrange the blankets swaddling her child in the old patrician's arms. Her fingers disappeared between the folds of the blankets and the harsh fabric of the formal frock coat; her shoe touched his. To her his breath smelled of flowers and four-poster beds.

With an uncharacteristic coyness only he could detect she stepped back to admire their accomplishment and the totally unfamiliar sight of her infant in the arms of a Deauville male. For a moment she found herself wondering why her husband had not been able to emulate his father; for a moment she

thought she knew what it might have been like if the
Old Gentleman and not the French-American horse-
breeder had fathered her fourth and final child on
her sturdy and receptive flesh. Her eyes met his;
he read her thoughts. She admired the youth in the
aged face and hands; she admired his rings confined
almost entirely to the right hand; she admired the
stick-pin which he wore in his cravat, a purple oval
on which an artist of no little skill had painted the
fawn-colored head of a dog. She who had only days
before determined that France was a nation of decadence now failed to see the Old Gentleman's resplen-
dent decadence. Now if she had had her choice she
would have exchanged without the slightest hesita-
tion her forty-four-year-old husband for his seventy-
six-year-old father, and in the moment of the
exchange it would have been as if the old patrician's
ninth son had never existed and as if she had always
been the wife of the loving and faithful father.
Again the Old Gentleman read her thoughts. There
he stood like a father. The deed was done.

Then Billy Boy awoke. Whether he awakened and
began immediately to scream, or in his sleep began
to scream and hence drove himself to furious wake-
fulness was not clear. But awake he was and screaming. The sounds that came from the tiny face just
visible beneath a fold of the topmost blue blanket
wrapped about the infant now in the Old Gentleman's charge were no sweet and appealing sounds

of a well-behaved baby in distress. Quite the contrary. Billy Boy was large for his eight months; he was possessed of Deauville lungs; his tiny face was now so fat as to appear eyeless, so round and wet and red with the blood of his anger as to appear on the verge of bursting. His screams had had no warning prelude; they were unremitting; they were as sustained and loud as a winter wind and filled the courtyard. The Old Gentleman heard the terrible screams in horror. He looked down at what he held in horror.

Heads turned. There was laughter. And on went Billy Boy, screaming precisely as if he knew why his mother had given him up and as if at eight months he could suddenly see himself at the age of thirty-two slumped over dead in the Stutz Bearcat. The pain of his screaming was like nothing the Old Gentleman or Irish matriarch or Uncle Jake had ever heard.

But what made the incident devastating to Uncle Jake was not merely that Billy Boy had awakened inopportunely, and was behaving badly, and was making of himself a humiliating spectacle, an overpowering spectacle, small as he was, and hence making a mockery of his three brothers if not all members of the Deauville family from America. The incident was devastating for Uncle Jake because of his mother.

Billy Boy was still at it, like some hateful screaming teakettle in human form. There were more titters,

more sounds of laughter. Uncle Jake knew that he
himself was smiling inanely and changing color. And
he was paralyzed in anguish and disbelief. He felt
that he and not his infant brother was the offender.
He watched in a state of abject silliness as the Old
Gentleman's face grew abruptly hard, as the Old
Gentleman's figure became as rigid as Billy Boy's
little wretched form, and as the Old Gentleman shot
to Uncle Jake a look of such disdain and accusation
that Uncle Jake found himself wishing, even at the
age of twelve, to bury his reddened face in his
mother's skirts and weep though he could not.

Abruptly the Old Gentleman rejected Billy Boy,
held him at arm's length, in severest anger thrust
him back into the arms of the stately but now
obviously stricken mother whom, thanks to the
squalling babe, the Old Gentleman no longer found
the least attractive. As she accepted back her child
the Irish matriarch looked the Old Gentleman full
in the face, understood what was happening, and
blanched. She did not much care that her child was
causing a disturbance or that the assembly found the
disturbance amusing. But she cared very much that
the Old Gentleman had responded to the baby's
screaming with revulsion, and that he held herself
to blame, and that he was now rejecting not the
impossibly screaming child but its mother. She
could hardly bear to have become so abruptly dim-
inished in the old patrician's eyes, precisely when

she too had thought that Billy Boy might bring them together, could hardly bear the Old Gentleman's abrupt and cruel denial when he had so obviously regarded her with interest and even affection only moments before.

Billy Boy was the darling of the American Deauvilles. Since his birth he had been chubby, good-humored, docile, never given to colic or the bad habits most infants form in their earliest hours. He was adored by his brothers and all the maids, and though Uncle Jake was his mother's favorite, still the Irish matriarch was proud and protective of her youngest, and enjoyed nothing more than nursing him, fondling him, and spending on him her new-found store of mother's love. She was proud of herself and of her infant and of being a mother. For eight months she had clung to Billy Boy and swathed him in the fullness of her matriarchal being. But now her mother's love had suffered a setback.

Now she confounded Uncle Jake by reversing herself, by becoming nothing like the mother he so depended upon and loved, by rejecting poor Billy Boy as strenuously as had the Old Gentleman. No sooner had she accepted again her child, with terrible brusqueness, then she turned to Uncle Jake and even as he drew back in alarm, thrust upon him the ignoble burden. The Irish matriarch did not deign to look Uncle Jake in the eye: she merely pushed the screaming baby into his arms, as if Uncle Jake were one of the maids and Billy Boy a viper, and turned away.

Uncle Jake loved Billy Boy as much as did his mother. But now he stood aghast and mortally distressed; now he himself was the bearer of what he thought of as the horrid burden; now he had been given sole responsibility for an infant whom even its mother could not tolerate or quiet. Could anything have been more unjust? And what could he do? How might he survive the laughter and the shrill noise which had reached its highest pitch and greatest intensity and was now piercing his ears, his breast, his very consciousness? He was alone; he was paralyzed; Billy Boy was hot and heavy and maddeningly loud in his arms.

Far on the other side of the crowd a footman opened the massive door into the chateau. The crowd parted. And somehow Uncle Jake began to move. He stumbled along with Billy Boy, attempting to greet the laughing onlookers with equanimity and at the same time to hush his brother by bouncing him and putting his own face to the little fat eyeless face from which came the screams. Billy Boy had freed one of his chubby arms; the tiny hand was in a fist and waving.

Uncle Jake reached the doorway, the footman smiled, Uncle Jake managed to step inside his grandfather's elegant chateau, where the light fell on an old suit of armor and on the hunting caps and whips eccentrically displayed around the marble-floored great hall. At once Billy Boy ceased his screaming and fell back into silence and deep sleep. The hot red color began to fade from the tiny face; contortion gave way to tranquility. And then there came the added relief of the youngest of the American maids who at that moment and on her own initiative appeared beside Uncle Jake in the otherwise empty foyer and took from Uncle Jake the sleeping babe.

"Poor Jake," whispered the pretty maid, standing close to him and looking up at him with her great silvery eyes, "you are a noble boy."

With those words there came to Uncle Jake a sudden rush of love for the maid, who was much smaller than he and only a few years his senior, and a sudden gratifying return of his love for Billy Boy. Instantly he felt only forgiveness for what Billy Boy had done and gratitude for the way the maid had come to his aid so swiftly, unobtrusively, sweetly. He loved them both.

Outside, the Old Gentleman was having a change of heart toward the Irish matriarch and was making amends. Again there was a cheerful hubbub in the courtyard, where the air was frosty and the light so clear and colorful that it might have been refracted through a heavenly prism.

To the pleasure of all concerned they had arrived.

The days that followed came to the visitors like
song birds to bits of varicolored glass in the sun.
The crisp fall weather held. Their accommodations
in the Old Gentleman's chateau followed exactly the
discreet and orderly arrangements of their shipboard
cabins, as if the Old Gentleman had somehow known
in advance his ninth son's domestic dilemmas and
had quite carefully placed the parents here, the sons
there, the secretary here and the maids down there
with the other domestics, thus assuring privacy and
decency to all. There were feasts, there were toasts,
one night they sat down to twenty geese, the next to
whole coveys of pheasants in hunter's sauce, the
next to a flock of roasted lambs. The pâtés, the
sherbets, the dishes of glazed fruits outdid by far
the dishes that the two French maids occasionally
prepared to the cook's disapproval at Deauville
Farms. The visitors were shown the countryside and
entertained by chamber ensembles and by male
singers whose basso voices might have belonged to
Deauville heirs, and by female singers whose
soprano voices were so pure and pleasing that
they quite disguised their unmistakably erotic
cast and gave virgin wings to their songs of
insinuation and desire. The Irish matriarch and her

mother-in-law did not know why they found the songs of the women singers so attractive, but so they did.

In the late mornings they all rode off to the hounds, except for the Irish matriarch and her mother-in-law, who followed the hunts in a light two-wheeled carriage. In the afternoons they strolled through the gardens, visited the chateaux of the Old Gentleman's nearest acquaintances. Darkness brought candlelight and celebrative meals and the inciting songs. Billy Boy was as good as gold; the Old Gentleman was kinder to Granny and tolerated Doc, and never again did he show to Uncle Jake his visage of inexplicable blame. Uncle Jake felt happier than he had ever been at Deauville Farms.

But the days of harmony and pleasure were further enhanced by certain occasions deemed by the Old Gentleman to be specially enjoyable to his assembly of delighted guests. The first took place before even a week had elapsed since their arrival.

One afternoon the bell in the Old Gentleman's private chapel began brightly ringing as for a wedding, and in the best of humors the Old Gentleman summoned everyone once more to the courtyard; with arms flung wide he herded them outdoors where they found awaiting them four rows of Empire chairs. The gilded frames and red plush cushions of the chairs shone in the agreeable light and contrasting as they did with the expanse of smooth and faintly

purple, faintly pink cobblestones, moved everyone
to exclamations of surprise and keen anticipation.
The boys and their mother were seated in the front
row.

Then the Old Gentleman gave a flourish with his
right hand, curving the open and graceful old hand
as might an impresario summoning an actor from his
place of concealment in the wings. And in response to
his flourish there came a tiny, sprightly clattering of
hooves and through the gateway rode a young girl
on a small and shapely dappled gray horse. Here
was a sight to win them all and audibly they sighed
and visibly they leaned forward. The girl, who was
the youngest child of the Old Gentleman's eighth
son, was the same age as Granny — fourteen — and
though she had been shyly present in the chateau
since this Deauville family reunion had commenced,
she had from time to time caught Uncle Jake's attention when he had seen her firm young face in the
candlelight, like a pale petal on a white china dish,
or had spied her slipping gracefully into seclusion
behind a mass of garrulous adults, still he had not
been prepared for the vision she now presented to
her already grateful audience. She looked like neither
boy nor girl or like the best of both. She wore a
trim black riding coat, a white stock, black boots
and a black skirt that reached to her ankles. Best of
all she wore a black silk hat which, befittingly small
to suit her little head, nonetheless called to mind the

larger and bolder silk hats generally worn by aristocratic men. Her dark brown hair was drawn tightly
to her head and arranged in a short plait that barely
touched the velvet collar of her coat. Around her
silk hat, which was tilted becomingly forward, was
tied a white silk ribbon that fluttered down the back
of her neck and provided exactly the right touch of
freedom and formlessness against the plait of hair.
She was wearing gray gloves and riding side-saddle.

As for her horse, its size could not have been
more appropriate to the size of its rider or its color
and markings more complementary to her costume.
The distance between the top of the girl's silk hat
and the saddle, which was hidden beneath the skirts
of the riding coat, was the same as from the saddle
to the brightly varnished black hooves that were
the size of teacups; when the breeze tossed up the
gray silken tail in a filmy plume of abandon, the
spread tail was a perfect counterpart to the horse's
head and neck and rose to the height of the little
creature's comely head. The gray mane was so long
that it echoed the tail; the black colorations of the
horse's legs were like tight stockings that mirrored
the prim costume of the rider. The small gray horse
looked like a hobbyhorse, its rider like a little man.
Yet the horse was filled with the supplest life and
no young girl could have sat upon its back more
decorously than did the daughter of the Old Gentleman's eighth son. Together they were toy-like and so

pretty that even the Old Gentleman in that moment
watched his granddaughter with admiration and not
the slightest sign of desire.

But the Old Gentleman had orchestrated the young
girl's exhibition, for so it was to be, in such a way as
to bring to absolute fruition the beauty of the young
girl and her steed. He had gone so far as to choose
the hour so that when the young girl stopped her
horse in the center of the courtyard, as now she
did, the sun was at such a distance above the westerly
wall as to make fall across the cobblestones the largest and longest possible shadow of horse and rider.
He had had the rows of chairs arranged at the eastern
end of the courtyard so that his audience faced not
only the girl and horse but, more important, the
shadow that made them one and the same. He had
even instructed his equestrienne to keep the head of
her mount facing to the north throughout the performance so that she presented to her audience only
her right side and never the left, and by so doing —
since both her legs were positioned on the left side of
the horse — created for her audience the illusion of a
legless rider seated in perfect balance upon her horse.
The fact that she appeared to have no legs was to the
entire ensemble as was the white ribbon affixed to
her hat: the incongruity without which the congru-
ous whole could not have achieved such perfection.

There sat Uncle Jake leaning forward in the front
row with his hands on his knees and his mouth

open; there before him were the performers, quite motionless but for the fluttering ribbon and the mane and tail stirring in the breeze. With shame he thought of himself and his shaggy and dumpy pony back at Deauville Farms; with helpless ardor he beheld in the girl and her gray horse a vision of poise such as he thought would never again be his to savor.

The exhibition began. The miniature portrait came to life. The young girl did not move so much as a finger, as far as Uncle Jake could see, but her steed responded to her invisible command: it cocked its right front leg and then the left. And again. The reins were gently curving from the young girl's lowered hands to the silver bit; she was applying no tension to the reins. Now the horse moved sideways three paces, no more and no less, in Uncle Jake's direction, and then returned to its starting place and stopped. Then it took three paces forward and returned. And then the small full-bodied animal and drummed with all four of its pretty hooves on the began to dance, as did the elongated shadow, cobblestones in a medley of pure obedience to the girl it bore. It danced, it drummed, it turned, but never so far as to destroy the illusion of its impossibly legless rider, and all the while the girl disguised as a little man did not move but remained ever and easily vertical and did not vary in any way her pretty posture as the horse continued to captivate hosts and visitors alike in its dance.

Nearly everyone in that audience rode horseback. Most of them were fox hunters. Their lives depended on horses, whether or not they hallooed while hurtling over high fences, and whether or not they loved their massive mounts as much as they did their own children. Some of them secretly feared past injuries and those to come; a few had little aptitude for riding. Yet for all of them their mares and geldings and fillies and stallions were a matter of course like stones in a brook or birds in the boughs. Most of the horses they bred and rode were large, rugged, unruly, brutish beasts of great stamina. The horses raced and hunted, pulled their carriages, carried them ambling through sylvan woods and took them cantering great distances. But little more. So here in the Old Gentleman's courtyard the spectacle of the young equestrienne and her gray horse schooled only in dressage appealed directly to what they knew and to their own relationships to horse and stable yet gave them all a taste of equestrian refinement that stirred them to surprise and pleasure. They had never thought of horsemanship as an art, but here indeed in the dancing horse they could see full well the refinement of an artist's mind.

As they waited, hoping the finals would never come, the Irish matriarch, who for days had regretted that her past refusal to ride with her husband now prevented her from joining the Old Gentleman in the hunting field and consigned her instead to the two-wheeled carriage driven by her mother-in-law and from which she could see little of the old and brave patrician, suddenly found herself constrained to whisper behind her hand to Uncle Jake.

"Jake," she whispered, "mark my words, dear boy. That child is dangerous."

He was stunned. He envied the girl, he likened her to their youngest maid, he loved her, he wanted to become her and take her splendid place on the gray horse, even though he had no use for horses. Surely the girl who might have been his sister could not in any way be sinister, as his mother had said. He was confident that there was nothing sinister about her.

But the Irish matriarch, who was proud of her self-control, did not know why she had been so suddenly stung to spite by a young horsewoman as clearly innocent as her own second son. So quickly she added in a gentler voice: "But she is a beautiful little rider, Jake. You might try to ride as well as she does. It would please your father."

In his relief he smiled, leaned briefly toward the once more reassuring bulk of his mother, and returned to concentrating on the girl and the bobbing and swaying horse.

Then came the finale.

All at once and above the dainty clatter of the hooves, they heard the loud and charming tinkling of a music box. Heads turned, a new and livelier surprise possessed the audience, the fact that they could not discover the source of the music, which was the essence of artificiality, added greatly to the effect. Thanks to its quick and pretty strains that were suggestive of the tips of quills picking silver strings as fine as hair, the horse's dance attained its childlike crescendo while the rider allowed herself the faintest smile. The tempo of the music began to slow, with no distortion of its tinkling notes, and with it slowed the dance of the gray horse. The slower the music, the slower the dance; and just as the even longer spaces between the notes caused each note to stand increasingly alone as if it were to be the only one struck on the scale of poignancy, so the modulation of the horse toward motionlessness brought to a head the lovely aching quality of its movements. Then the music ceased, leaving behind its song in the silence, and the horse and rider grew so still that they might have been waxen figures in an equestrian museum. And then, with a slowness that brought everyone to the edge of his seat, the gray horse bowed. Out went its front legs, down came the head and neck and chest, lower and lower in the greatest possible contrast to the vertical line of the young girl, until the audience could no longer bear the nearly human tribute paid to it by the little horse and broke out in sustained and mellifluous applause. At once the animal returned to its proper stance, the girl laughed, and horse and rider backed out of the courtyard and disappeared through the gate.

As one the audience rose to its feet, still clapping. They exclaimed aloud to each other, while clapping, and smiles vied with smiles and no one had praise enough for the exhibition which had taught them all that artificiality not only enhances natural life but defines it. Footmen came with trays of sherry, and the sunlight deepened, the voicing of appreciation grew softer, more lyrical. The Irish matriarch looked about for the Old Gentleman while Uncle Jake stayed close to her side and thought of the girl in the long skirts and black silk hat.

Then the Old Gentleman appeared and as one the audience realized that though they had all seen him act the impresario and with his raised hand start the performance, still he had not taken one of the red plush chairs for himself, had not remained with them in the courtyard, had not been a passive witness to his granddaughter's exhibition. He was smiling broadly; he was perspiring; clearly he expected thanks. In all this the truth was evident: that not only had he himself orchestrated the day, but that it was he who had taught the girl dressage, and he who had from a little balcony conducted her performance and determined her every move, and he who had turned the handle of the music box. Never had the old patrician looked younger or more pleased with himself.

Weeks later, in the final days of their visit, when the Irish matriarch had learned well her lesson about the Old Gentleman and had suffered once more the full brunt of disillusionment, she remembered this afternoon of the dancing horse and thought, with a return of her terrible grimness, that even a lecherous man can be seduced into a state of the purest innocence.

Still the autumn weather held. The chestnuts fell, the woodlands turned a golden red, the hunting and feasting and visiting continued. Uncle Jake took a keener interest in riding. Whenever and wherever possible he avoided the hazards of jumping fences, going far out of his way to discover gates through which he could pass with care and safety, and yet his determination to trail the hunt and not be left entirely behind increased. Occasionally he was rewarded by the briefest glimpse of the young equestrienne soaring as dangerously as the rest of them over some high obstacle of hedge or stone or rail, the white ribbon flashing from the black silk hat, her hunting whip cruelly punishing the flanks of a gigantic brown gelding that was one of the largest and most unruly brutes in the field. Doc and Granny had nothing like Uncle Jake's incentive to pursue the hunt and so each morning slipped away as soon as they could and hid themselves and their ponies amongst the frosted trees where they were spared the thundering of the horses or the sound of their father's voice booming above all others in pursuit of the fox.

Jouncing along in the two-wheeled carriage, the Irish matriarch sought to win her mother-in-law's approval and to conceal her happiness whenever the Old Gentleman galloped across her line of sight, his red coat ablaze and long face flushed joyously in the madness of the chase he led. The Irish matriarch wanted nothing more than to take the place of the mysterious woman who, on a large horse that resembled an immense white stag, was never far from the Old Gentleman, turning and wheeling as he turned and wheeled, jumping and racing as he jumped and raced, still the Irish matriarch did her best to put the clearly favored woman out of mind, just as she put out of mind her husband's red-headed secretary who rode after him with the same tenacity and prerogative with which the mysterious woman rode after the Old Gentleman. It did not occur to her that the key to the mysterious woman was the red-headed secretary, or could not allow herself to apply what she knew about the red-headed secretary to the mysterious woman. The analogy would have exposed the Old Gentleman for what he was, whereas now she lived only for what she thought him to be. As for the Irish matriarch's own husband, he rode with such recklessness that he fell from his mount far more frequently than did his brothers, and each of his nearly disastrous falls, from which he arose refreshed and laughing, was, for the Irish matriarch, a diversion she welcomed almost as much as the sudden sight of the Old Gentleman putting bloody spurs to his horse or sounding his brass horn. Daily she wished her husband a fatal injury; daily and silently she urged the Old Gentleman to even greater feats among his sons. Uncle Jake felt only confusion and dismay whenever he came upon his father sprawled in a shocking tangle of hooves and reins; he wished that his father might be more careful.

On they went in pursuit of the fox and their various desires, while the hounds turned the countryside to music and the rigor of the days gave way to the gaiety of the nights.

At the end of October there came the message the Old Gentleman had been eagerly awaiting: the grapes, much later than usual, were ready at last for harvesting. Each fall the happy news was brought from the Old Gentleman's nearby farm by an elderly retainer whose infectious pleasure was a source of special amusement and good cheer for the Old Gentleman.

When the grapes were ready it was urgent that they be picked at once lest they be destroyed by over-ripeness of a sudden change in the weather; nothing was more satisfying to the Old Gentleman and hence to all those who lived and worked for the sake of his well-being than the successful harvesting

of the grapes. The quality of life in the Old Gentleman's chateau depended on the quality of the wine at
rest in his cellars; the quality of the wine depended
on the Old Gentleman's judgment. He it was for
whom the grape was grown and the grape was as
much his province as was the horse. He had written
but a single line of verse in his lifetime and it was
this line, and this line alone, that appeared on the
labels affixed to the bottles of each fall's harvest:
"Without the sun I am nothing." There was no one
in the chateau or its vicinity who did not want the
Old Gentleman to have his sun. So the time of
harvesting was a time of rejoicing and hard work,
and no sooner had the elderly retainer announced
that the moment was now at hand, thereby signaling
the spectacle of the sun's fruition and the end of a
season than everything that was done and said in the
Old Gentleman's chateau reflected the intensity and
spirit of all those directly concerned with the grape
itself. Just as the Old Gentleman orchestrated the
hunt and had orchestrated his youngest granddaughter's exhibition of dressage, so, for his guests, he
orchestrated the treading of the grapes. At his bidding the elderly retainer drove his lumbering wooden
cart directly from the chateau to the village and there
alerted the village virgins to the special importance of
this year's event. Not a girl in the village could boast
of purity. But for the Old Gentleman's present pur-
poses they were all village virgins, and so at his com-

mand they were, though if he had given the matter
his full attention the Old Gentleman would have finally recognized which among their number he had
himself deflowered.

On the very day that followed the arrival of the
happy news the Old Gentleman led his privileged
party off to the farm. They went on horseback and
in open carriages, the servants riding in great wooden
carts which the Old Gentleman had summoned from
the farm and which were drawn by the shaggiest and
most majestic work horses kept in his barns. At the
last moment the Irish matriarch requested that Jake,
her favorite, be allowed to accompany herself and her
mother-in-law in the two-wheeled carriage, and so
Uncle Jake gratefully left his hateful pony to a young
groom and joined the two courtly women in their
little carriage with its wicker body and lacquered
wheels. His grandmother drew him once to her bosom
despite his large size while his mother put her arm
through his and pressed her warmth against him.
For weeks Uncle Jake and his brothers had generally
been denied their mother's comforting presence which
Uncle Jake had sorely missed; now he had been
restored to her and restored as well to his grandmother, whose very unfamiliarity and greater age
made her all the more endearing, though the light in
her eyes was not the light of affection, as he assumed,
but rather the anger she felt towards her daughter-
in-law for contaminating this close space with a male.

Uncle Jake smelled their womanhood and admired their thick tresses piled up on their heads and began to think of himself as having two mothers and the love of both. He knew that despite his size he was riding with them not as their protector but as the one protected, not as their symbolic manly companion but as their child. He did not know how short-lived this rare sensation would prove to be. On their ponies his brothers trotted along behind the carriage and bore as best they could their envy.

That early afternoon the sun hung low overhead like an immense blood orange, so fat and self-contained that the clear light of the hour seemed to contradict the smoldering sun and to have an earthly rather than heavenly source. The singing of the grape pickers reached the privileged party before the pickers themselves came into sight. The invisible singers sounded like school children; their music was a welcome novelty after the daily strident music of the hounds. Then the privileged party topped a small rise and saw the exact pictorial equivalent of the grape picker's rustic song: the cluster of barns the color of old leather; the small vineyard bursting with blue grapes and green leaves; the high wooden horse-drawn carts standing here and there between the rows and bearing the great baskets brimming with a harvest so shiny and deeply blue that even the uninitiated understood at once that the separation of grape and stem had just the moment before occurred; and finally the pickers themselves, the boys and old men, the wives and husbands and aged women all bent of back and moving down the rows and singing or pausing to drink the new wine that was being passed among them in thick tumblers.

Uncle Jake had never seen the sea of living blue with its green ripples; he had never seen so many workers in a field and so bent over that they looked like beetles; he had never seen a field of half-intoxicated grape pickers, which is what they were, and found himself yearning for his own sip of the wine. He thought that his own blueberries had become his grandfather's grapes; he thought that the prickly blueberry bushes of Deauville Farms had become his grandfather's vineyard.

The privileged party alighted in the barnyard, filling it with festive chaos. Sleek ducks scampered from under the hooves and wheels and patent leather boots. Scented ladies walked on earth freshly cleared of manure. Wisps of floating straw clung to silk. The largest of the barns, an enormous stone structure with a steeply pitched roof of blackened wood, awaited them with open doors. It was, as the Old Gentleman said, their provincial opera house, and grandly he stood aside and encouraged them all to enter. They did so, and their exclamations were louder, more lyrical, more surprised than they had been on the first such enjoyable occasion when they

had taken their places in the courtyard of the Old
Gentleman's chateau. The spectacle was as intoxicating as the wine that was its final product: from the
rude beams high above their heads hung cluster
upon tied cluster of grapes that were drying into
raisins; three stone treading troughs rectangular in
shape and large enough to hold six persons each
were situated against the right-hand longest wall; the
barefooted village virgins were huddled in a far
corner and giggling; and most remarkable of all, there
faced the treading troughs a gigantic stage built on
order of the Old Gentleman and bearing, also according to his instructions, the same four rows of
Empire chairs, with their gilt frames and cushions of
red plush, that had awaited them all on that now
distant day in the courtyard. The incongruity between the chairs, the treading troughs, the rude
beams, and the giggling girls attempting to put on
the shy and lively air of virgins was more magical
than the poignant incongruity originally created by
the young equestrienne and her gray horse. Servants
moved among the visitors with trays of wine; the
village virgins wore only short blue smocks that
showed their knees; the whitewashed interior of the
barn smelled strongly of the musty, earthen, sunny
smell of the fresh grape, the crushed grape, the
dried grape, smelled of all the harvests of the past
and the one commencing. Here then was the fount

of the Old Gentleman's well-being, the place of the grape, the cool and timeless opera house, as he called it, of his life's vintage.

Granny and Doc and Uncle Jake were offered and accepted small glasses of their grandfather's wine of several seasons past, and it was in fact the Old Gentleman himself who removed Uncle Jake's glass from the servant's tray and placed it in the hand of his grandson. The wine was clear, cool, light red in color, and high in alcoholic content. With the first sip Uncle Jake became agreeably dizzy; through the intoxicating smell of the wine came the pungent smell of the pipe smoke that lingered always about the person of the old patrician. It was only now after weeks of discomfort among his rowdy uncles and the father and grandfather whom he both revered and feared that Uncle Jake began to yield at last to the temptations of the masculine sensibility, though the ordinary evils of manhood were not for Uncle Jake's attaining.

The old patrician called for attention.

"Ladies and gentlemen," he said in the abrupt and timeless silence, and raising his glass and putting his arm around Uncle Jake's shoulders, "it is a pleasure to receive you here in this lowly barn. I am only a provincial aristocrat, an old man who has not once set foot in a railway train and never will, and who has not seen Monsieur Eiffel's handiwork and never will. The Deauville family itself is provincial: we live only to honor our horses, our women, and our grapes. Our horses are famed for their hot blood; our women are justly famed for the number of sons they are capable of bearing in a lifetime; our grapes — the very grapes which at my signal shall fill these now empty treading troughs — are famous throughout this region for imparting to the wine we make each year a flavor which is best described as the flavor of our moral heritage. It is the flavor of the Deauville line itself. As we all know, the ancients discovered the mysteries of the grape. There is no religion, no ceremony, no banquet that can do without the grape. The grape has always been taken to represent the boldness of the sun and the blood of our gods. And so it is with the Deauvilles. 'Nothing Too Much,' our family motto says, and regarding the horse, the honored woman, and the grape, ours is a morality of excess. 'Without the Sun I am Nothing,' as I myself have written, but the true meaning of my single line of verse lies in its unwritten corollary: 'In My Birth I am All.' Excess, my dears, excess. In our provincial wine there flows the blood of excess.

"Now, my dears, please join me in a toast. Let us now honor, in all our Deauville excessiveness, those two ladies who amongst all our ladies here present were the first and last so far to assume our family name. The one has borne but half the children of the other, yet surely we must all agree that theirs is the motherhood that most triumphantly preserves our blood, our morality, our honor.

"My dears, once again I ask you to drink to the health of my beloved wife and equally beloved daughter-in-law from across the seas!"

They drank in silence, with renewed exclamations of surprise they broke that same silence as they might have broken their glasses which were rapidly refilled. Uncle Jake felt the Old Gentleman's arm tighten across his shoulders and through a clear and pinkish film thought to himself that this handsome tribute to his mother could not have been paid had not his father brought them all to France.

The Old Gentleman called out again and asked them to take their places on the stage. And now his orchestrative powers were more pervasive than ever, since now the audience found itself remarkably and unaccountably divided, the men in the first two rows and the women in the last two rows, though they had not received any prior instructions or been ushered to their chairs. It was as if the Old Gentleman's toast to two women had sent each and every man in the privileged party to obtain for himself a seat affording the best view of what was about to occur in the treading troughs. And which of them sat in the center of the first row? Why, Uncle Jake himself, who had no idea of why he had the place of honor in a sea of men, or of why he now found

himself flanked by father and grandfather both, as if
they meant once and for all to crush his shyness
between them, and to offer him up as the purest
sacrifice to their gender, and so to impart to their
victim the massive cache of sex that was not his but
theirs. Uncle Jake had wished for a sip of wine. His
wish had been more than granted. Now he knew
that he was more than half drunk on embarrassment
and pride.

The Old Gentleman clapped his hands three times
in a prearranged signal. Four violinists, until now
unseen in the shadows of the corner opposite from
the village virgins, flung up their violins and bows
and commenced a tune so swiftly paced that it made
Uncle Jake dizzier than had the wine and set his
knees to jiggling. At the sound of the tune the first
in the long line of grape pickers that had formed in
the barnyard entered through the high doors and
emptied her basket into the treading trough nearest
the virgins. In most cases the baskets were taller
than those who carried them; the grapes came crest-
ing from each basket as from a horn of plenty.

The music played on, the mountains of blue grapes
rose higher than the walls of the treading troughs
which were kneehigh and discolored with the juices
of vintages of other years. Uncle Jake leaned forward so as not to miss one detail of the provincial
pageantry which his grandfather, like an old master,
had created; he was aware that the two colossal men

who flanked him were focusing their attention as much on himself as on the scene before them. His pleasure, he understood, was theirs.

Again the old patrician clapped his hands three times. The treading troughs were filled. The now empty-handed grape pickers pressed themselves to the whitewashed walls. The music stopped, and in the silence the Old Gentleman got to his feet.

"Ladies and gentlemen," he said, "it is well known that the headiest of wines cannot possibly come into being unless the grape is crushed by the bare and tender feet of a virgin. Men and boys, old women and impure girls tread the grapes from which we make our lesser wines. But the virgin girl imparts to our best wine her very innocence; it is her own virginity she crushes when she treads the grape. And so I give you eighteen village virgins whose only love so far is for the fruit of my fields! Virgins, ladies and gentlemen, the pick of our village virgins!"

The violinists swept into another tune still more conducive than the first to the general mood of pastoral abandon. There was clapping. And now the village virgins swarmed forward. Each leapt nimbly and prettily to her place in one of the treading troughs until each trough contained six girls who were one and all consumed by the Old Gentleman's ardor for the sacred grape. They laughed, they danced, with arms about each other's shoulders they turned in fast circles, then singly hopped high in

the air, arms reaching and curving above their heads,
blue skirts flying about their thighs. With naked feet
they crushed the grapes. The juice of the crushed
grapes spurted and splattered, lodging in their heads
of uncovered hair, wetting their faces and their simple smocks and causing them to wipe their eyes.
And still they turned, still pumped themselves up
and down in the rising tide of grapes already crushed
and fresh grapes bobbing on the froth.

Uncle Jake leaned forward. He watched, he listened. And then to his utter astonishment and the
surprise of everyone else there occurred that *piece de
resistance*, as the Old Gentleman called it beneath
his breath, which no member of the audience could
have predicted. Without a sign from the Old Gentleman, without the signal of his clapping hands, with
no apparent prompter to enable them to act in unison,
nonetheless at this precise moment and in fact in
unison the village virgins suddenly stripped away
their simple smocks, tossed them in random heaps
on the stone floor beyond the troughs. In the instant
and while preserving perfectly their rhythm they
achieved completely the freedom and innocent nudity
promised by the virgin state.

Uncle Jake was stunned. His jaw went slack. Dis-
tinctly he heard his mother's gasp of horror though
she was seated far behind him in the last row of
chairs and though the girls were laughing and the
amorous voices of the violins were increasing in vol-

ume as well as in tempo. It had not yet occurred to Uncle Jake that girls of his own age could ever go unclothed or that they were the possessors of sweet immature bodies that could in fact be bared. Yet here it was, the very flesh of girlhood, and he did not know where to look or which nude girl was the prettiest. He saw unthinkable little buttocks, bare arms, young legs softer and smoother and whiter by far than his own; he saw their little breasts for which he had no word; he saw their sloping shoulders and stomachs like small puddings in shallow bowls. And every time he made his selection, and in shame and eagerness chose this or that bouncing figure as the object of his suddenly shocked and boundless curiosity, some different virgin girl caught his eye as a more rewarding object of his attention. Time, he knew, was short; he must trust his judgment, force himself to fix his gaze on but one of the eighteen girls if he was to see what he now wanted desperately to see—or else lose this opportunity forever in the frenzied blur of their bodies. Already those bodies were dripping and darkening with the juice of the grape; soon the flashes of white skin would be clothed in tight skins of purplish blue.

And still the Old Gentleman had more tricks with which to beguile his favorite grandson, because just as Uncle Jake was succumbing to despair, unable to control his turning head and wayward glances, suddenly his choice was made. Suddenly he saw directly in front of him in the middle treading trough, as if

for his eyes alone, the young equestrienne divested
of her black silk hat and trimly tailored black riding
coat and skirt. She had been there all along, of course,
thoroughly disguised in her blue smock. Of course
she was not a village virgin, yet virgin she was, as
the seventeen other girls were not. In her nakedness
she revealed to Uncle Jake a slight body worthy of
the richest convent. And yet the roundness of her
limbs and torso cried out for the couch. Her hair once
so tightly bound was down; of all the treaders she
danced with the highest and most exaggerated steps
around and around the trough through the thick
sea of grapes.

"So, my dear grandson," whispered the Old Gentleman behind a hand, and leaning unashamedly
close to Uncle Jake, "there she is: my youngest
granddaughter treading grapes with the children of
farmers at my behest and as my gift to you. She
knows that you are watching which is why she
stripped off her smock with such abandon and why
she frolics before your eyes with such gusto. I had
assumed, quite rightly I see, that you were as yet
unfamiliar with the nudity of women. I may tell you
that my granddaughter's fair young body has never
until this moment been looked upon by man or boy.
Now she bares herself in a host of men but only for
you. She displays her nakedness for you, my dear,
for you. And I see by your color, my dear boy, that
you appreciate my gift. I cannot ask for more."

So thanks to his grandfather Uncle Jake's choice

was made. Now he had eyes only for the young
equestrienne. Now he could study her at will and for
as long as her virgin energy lasted His concen-
tration was unbroken, the seventeen other girls were
to him no more than towels flapping on a line. He
hardly saw them, he was not tempted to look away
from the innocent forwardness of his French cousin.

But even his grandfather could not entirely control
the events of that afternoon. Suddenly behind them
came a stir in the audience, and then a commotion,
and before their heads could turn, down rushed the
youngest American maid, laughing and frantically
stripping off her clothes and underclothes as she ran.
She tore the white cap from her head but forgot one
black garter that ringed a bare thigh; her blonde hair
was as pale as the autumn moon; her breasts, when
she freed them, were clearly the breasts of a mature
woman. Here was no virgin and certainly no village
virgin, as everyone could see, and yet her defiance of
the myth of purity for the sake of attempting pub-
licly to please the Old Gentleman was in itself heroic.
She vaulted into the middle treading trough and,
by doing so, quite overshadowed the sweet antics of
the young equestrienne. Once more Uncle Jake was
thrown into confusion, and in the most enjoyable
kind of misery he gave himself over to looking upon
the shocking nudity of the newcomer. After all, their
youngest maid was not only an adult, despite her
youth, but was also a person whom he had respected

and obeyed since first she had arrived at Deauville Farms; she had always been especially comforting to him and hence inaccessible. Now her nudity was more than shocking; hers was the violation of a strict taboo. He stared, he bit his lip, his admiration was such that he could not breathe. There was a scattering of male laughter and applause above the music and cries of the girls.

Uncle Jake heard his grandfather's voice, felt the old patrician leaning across him and momentarily blocking his view. "Well," said the old patrician to Uncle Jake's father, "she is quite as much at home in the trough as she is in the bed," and chuckling to himself sat once more upright with folded arms to enjoy the spectacle of the young maid who could not speak French. As for Uncle Jake, it made no difference to him that he did not understand his grandfather's remark.

When the festival of the day was over, and the grapes were crushed and the juices drained, and all the grape treaders had fled to another and smaller barn where they washed themselves in buckets of cold water and modestly attired themselves once more, and when the fair audience flocked again to the barnyard, Uncle Jake was pleased to find himself still flanked by his father and grandfather. It did not matter that Granny and poor Doc were nowhere to be seen; he was quite capable of standing alone between his father and grandfather. Thanks to them

there were no prohibitions, he had drunk wine and
survived this day. The old barn had not fallen about
his shoulders as he had thought it might. He was
proud of himself.

But he had not reckoned on the Irish matriarch.
Now he saw her pushing through the crowd. He saw
the squared shoulders, the stern face, the flying hat,
the sweeping skirts, the message of the great bosom.
A strand of her wonderfully thick hair had come
loose, the stern face was white. The handsome Irish
features had been sculpted by the hand of fury. She
had seen them — himself and his father and grandfather—now she was bearing down on them and could
not be stopped. His father's face assumed a quizzical
expression; his grandfather's face relaxed into an expression of surprise and welcome as if the approach-
ing woman's wrath was to him a matter of no con-
sequence at all.

"My daughter-in-law from across the seas," he
said in his gentlest tone and looked at the Irish
matriarch with familial affection and with a bright-
ness of a more personal kind.

"Monsieur," came the cold and quivering voice,
"how could you . . . "

"Madame?"

"Oh, Monsieur, my poor boy . . . "

"Here you see him, Madame. Why 'poor'?"

She waited, standing so close to Uncle Jake that
though his mother had not yet deigned to look at

him, nonetheless he felt himself accused by her dark eyes. Helplessly and in silence he appealed to his father, whose long face was hard; in apprehension he sought the face of his grandfather, whose equanimity betrayed a hint of amusement. Again he turned to his mother, from whom there was no escape, and now in the white face the cheeks were reddening, and now the great bosom that had been still was heaving. Those nearby were beginning to stare; the sun that had been smoldering before they had entered the barn now sat directly overhead. Where now was the wine, the laughter, the music of the violins, the atmosphere in which the baseness of his curiosity had been condoned? Again his mother was speaking and her hurt was audible even to himself beneath the ice of her anger.

"Monsieur," she said, faltering, "I cannot believe . . . I would not have believed . . . that you . . . that you of all people . . . could corrupt his innocence . . . . "

"But Madame," said the Old Gentleman after a pause, "my dear, my dearest daughter-in-law, you are mistaken. This is 1892, and the innocent ritual you have just been witness to is an established one. Why, each year the village virgins come to me and . . . "

"Stop!" cried the Irish matriarch in a whisper. "I will not hear it . . . I will not see again those sights!"

"Madame," said the Old Gentleman slowly and less patiently, "I regret that you found the young women offensive. They were not meant to be. They are only the lilies of my vintage . . . . "

"Naked," said the Irish matriarch, "naked . . . . "

"In France," said the Old Gentleman, "we do not hide our lilies."

"Your own granddaughter," said the Irish matriarch, "and my own maid!"

"Madame," said the Old Gentleman softly, "I am not to answer for your maid."

"Monsieur," said the Irish matriarch, whose anger had been suddenly restored, "you have corrupted my son. And as for you, Sir," she said, glancing briefly and disdainfully at her husband, "you have drunk too much wine!" Before his father or grandfather could reply and aware that his mother had still not once looked his way, Uncle Jake heard her sharp command and shuddered.

"Come with me, Jake, "she said. "At once."

She turned on her heel and strode toward the two-wheeled carriage where her mother-in-law, who feigned to be as affronted as her daughter-in-law, sat waiting. Close behind the Irish matriarch walked Uncle Jake. He heard the crowd's laughter as he had so painfully heard it weeks before. And now he himself had become the squalling Billy Boy of that distant day.

That night, while Uncle Jake lay sleepless, the Irish matriarch spent long hours in her mother-in-law's bedchamber and there received the full brunt of her disillusionment.

And that night, in the company of the mysterious woman and the red-headed secretary, the Old Gentleman and his ninth son well rewarded the youngest American maid for her irrepressible contribution to the day's events.

The bottles produced that day became the Old Gentleman's private stock which in future years he drank alone or solely with the mysterious woman. In future years the old man never drank that wine without laughing.

The weather turned. The leaves fell, the temperature dropped, intermittent rain came down. They had harvested the grapes just in time: another few days and the entire crop would have been lost, the Old Gentleman would have been denied the sun and the Irish matriarch would have retained her peace of mind at least for a while longer. Now her disillusionment had as great an effect on hosts and guests as did the bad weather. She was sulking. Her mother-in-law, who had not at all meant to confess the full history of her martyrdom down to the present, had lost control of herself and revealed the longtime misery of her situation only because of the flaring up of her daughter-in-law's temper. She could not resist flaunting in the face of her daughter-in-law

her own marital disgrace, compared to which the
sight of a few naked girls was nothing. Not only had
the Irish matriarch to contend with the horrors that
had been told her by the older woman, but she had
also to contend with the pride that prevented her
from sharing her own dark secrets with her mother-
in-law and to contend with the anger she felt toward
her mother-in-law for destroying the grandeur
of the Old Gentleman and hence snuffing out in one
night of talking the younger woman's only chances
for a moment of grand passion. And of course the
mother-in-law was equally angry at the Irish matriarch for what that younger woman now knew.
Yet each had none but the other to turn to. They
walked arm-in-arm together; they refused to ride
in the wicker carriage to the hunt; they withdrew
for days and nights on end to irritate and console
each other before the roaring fire in the Frenchwoman's bedchamber. Squalls and gales and bursts
of sleeting rain and the heaviest frosts to date were
nothing compared with the sullenness of those two
grandes dames in the Old Gentleman's chateau. The
worst of it was that they had both been secretly
pleased by the Old Gentleman's toast in the barn,
and knew that now there would be no more toasts
for them.

The worse their tempers and the weather, the
more virulent and lighthearted the Old Gentleman
became. He and his ninth son were equally aware

that there could be no appeasing that indomitable
Frenchwoman who was the wife of the one and
mother of the other. They did not even try to
appease her. But the Old Gentleman still had hopes
of bringing to bed the fine figure of his daughter-
in-law from across the seas and so did what he
could to mollify her anger and diminish the harsh
effects of her disillusionment. Even should he be
unsuccessful in luring forth his daughter-in-law's
carnality which he thought of as a dark rose as
big as a cabbage, still he liked her well enough to
do his best to lift from her handsome shoulders the
pathetic burden placed upon them by his spiteful
wife. He spoke to his daughter-in-law discreetly;
the baritone singers he hired began subtly to address
their songs to her; he caused his cooks to prepare
her favorite dishes. In all this his ninth son knew
enough to stand aside and not further ruffle the
dark waters. He wished his father well. But the Irish
matriarch was aghast at the Old Gentleman's attentions and niceties and made her angry bosom more
prominent and her jaw more firm.

Uncle Jake thought that he was the cause of the
bad weather and his mother's unhappiness. He
thought that he had lost his mother's love forever.
Whenever he could he timidly courted his mother
but to no avail. He could no longer bear the touch of
Billy Boy and so Granny, who had become both bored
and bewildered in the Old Gentleman's chateau and

did not appreciate French cooking, assumed as much
as he could the care of his infant brother and spent
long hours carrying the heavy baby up and down the
cold corridors.

The five American maids were on their best be-
havior though the youngest could not believe her
good fortune and showed it. The two French maids,
ever loyal to their French-American master, clucked
their tongues and shook their heads at this sad turn
of events.

The Old Gentleman had long intended that the
third and last of those occasions which he had deemed
to be specially conducive to the felicity of all his
guests would be in still greater honor of the horse.
He wanted the horse itself to close dramatically the
circle opened so prettily by the daughter of his
eighth son; he wanted his audience to experience
nothing less than the life and mystery of the horse
as he himself had always known it. At exactly the
time when he wished her to, his favorite brood mare
came into heat.

Now the familiar four rows of chairs were set out
at one end of the arena in the Old Gentleman's
stable which in itself resembled a small chateau and
was separated only by another and lesser courtyard
from the elegant chateau it mirrored. The oval arena

that formed the central portion of the stable was used for the breeding and training of the Old Gentleman's horses, and was well known around the countryside as serving occasionally as a dining room for the Old Gentleman and his sons. Its flooring was a carpet of soft dark earth; around its whitewashed walls were hung greater-than-life-sized portraits of illustrious mares and stallions done in oils; above each portrait was a high leaded window that let in vast quantities of light. Four fireplaces, each larger than a standing horse, provided warmth. The corridors that radiated from the arena and down which were located the box stalls twice the size of ordinary stalls and paneled in mahogany and teak, could be closed off by curtains of red velvet. Now all but one of the curtains were drawn and the fires lit.

Thus the scene that greeted the privileged audience when the Old Gentleman ushered them into the oval arena was stranger by far than that of Empire chairs in a sunny courtyard or Empire chairs arranged on a large and makeshift stage in a barn. This scene provided far more incongruity than they had yet been treated to, so that the voicing of their expectations might understandably have reached a new crescendo. But it did not. That which was most surprising kept them silent: namely, the sight of the brood mare and her aged groom standing stock still in the center of the otherwise empty arena. Gray light came down

upon them from the high windows; the light from the
four fires was as bright as the sun; the lone horse
and patient groom stood facing each other.

"To your places, to your places, ladies and gentlemen," called the old patrician, and in the surprising
silence his tone of voice was gentle and sad, soft
with suppressed affection for his horse, his groom,
his audience.

Silently the assembled company obeyed, but ran-
domly, with unexpected confusion. Again Uncle Jake
found himself in the front row; nowhere could he
see his father; he was not to enjoy the protection of
his grandfather who now stood apart from them
all beside the aged groom. The Irish matriarch and
her mother-in-law had let it be known that they
would not attend this day's event. Still a host of
women and not men now surrounded Uncle Jake and
added greatly to his consternation. Why had so
many unfamiliar women crowded to the first row of
chairs? And what was it about the patient horse
that made him so apprehensive? Suddenly he stole a
secret glance toward his left-hand side. Someone
had just sat down beside him, and it was none
other than the young equestrienne, the very person
whose bareness he had beheld with such dire con-
sequences. At his side the young equestrienne sat
expressionless, unperturbed, sublimely modest. She
neither spoke to him nor glanced at him nor in any
way acknowledged him. Her folded hands were

faintly pink in color, his were a chalky white. Her gown was blue; her dark brown hair was once more plaited in the chignon which he remembered from the day when she had sat upon her dancing horse; her face in profile was an ivory cameo created by an artist with an eye for pride. But why did he feel such faint and disagreeable surges of shame at the sight of this new horse that had brought them once more together? He did not know.

The old patrician spoke. "Ladies and gentlemen," he said, "behold this horse. My dears, she is my favorite brood mare and with good reason. We are all aware of those defects that plague the horse that has been poorly bred — pawing, rushing, backing, biting, kicking, head tossing, taking the bit in her teeth, putting her head to the wind. Oh my dears, what could be worse than generations of poor breeding? But in this horse we have not a single defect. Quite the opposite. Symmetry, my dears, and balance," continued the old patrician, slowly circling the ancient groom and the oddly patient horse at which he gently and proudly gestured while he spoke, "symmetry and balance. For these she was created. For these she lives. Note well her head which is in direct proportion to the neck and is not too heavy nor too small; see the neck, which is long and muscular and flexible; look at her deep broad chest and well-sprung ribs, the loins that are short and strong, the hindquarters that are wide and symmetrical. Yes,

my dears, note well the glorious muscles of these
hindquarters that are so nicely rounded. Oh my
dears," said the Old Gentleman, reaching up and
gently stroking the broad nose, "she is a creature of
intelligence, of the most refined and delicate sort of
intelligence. I have only to mention that she was
sired by the great Harpagon to give you an indication
of her character."

Here the Old Gentleman stepped back from the
waiting horse, looked upwards, clasped his hands
behind his back, laughed softly and fell to musing.
Then he continued.

"Here before us stands Harpagon's direct descendant. The nobility that was Harpagon's is hers. 'No
feet, no horse,' is the old adage and here we have
four perfect feet squarely planted beneath her body
and pointing straight ahead. And look at her tail; if
I gathered up the luxury of this creature's tail its
silky profusion would overflow my arms! Nothing
alive is more familiar to me than this brood mare, or
more important. She is covered only by stallions of
lineage, and she is covered by no stallion that is not
my own. I am in personal attendance when she is
covered, I am in personal attendance on each foal
she drops. She is a Thoroughbred, my dears, a
Thoroughbred. As are we all!

"And now." said the Old Gentleman, once more
standing aside and wiping his brow, "now let her
be covered!"

The privileged audience could no longer maintain its silence or contain its thrill, and began to murmur. Uncle Jake who had not understood half of what his grandfather had been saying, leaned forward and stared at the large brown horse at which his grandfather was still pointing with an imperious arm. The young equestrienne said nothing and made not a sound. As for the brood mare herself, she did not know that now her odd patience was to be rewarded and stood as she had been standing since first the privileged audience had laid eyes upon her: with her front legs somewhat forward and slightly spread; with her hind legs thrust to the rear and widely spread; and with the tail, which the Old Gentleman had praised so highly, lifted well above the straining hindquarters and swung to the side. She was patient; the heat that inflamed her from within shone in her coat; she was braced not for what she feared but for what she desired.

From far down that single corridor from the mouth of which the red curtains were tightly drawn there came the piercing sound that thrilled still more the privileged audience but shocked and frightened Uncle Jake. It was a trumpeting that could not have been made by any musical instrument, a shrieking that could not have come from the throat of a human no matter its similarity to a human cry. Again they heard it, and closer, and then, accompanied by his frantic groom, into the oval arena lunged the long-awaited stallion with tossing head, rolling eye, flying hooves, jaws wide. He kicked, he strained, he foamed, his brown coat was drenched in his desperation.

"But look there," called the Old Gentleman, who was now perspiring as freely as the stallion, "he sees her! And watch what he does, my dears. Look closely. This stallion would kill his groom in order to mount my favorite brood mare. He smells her, yet he so heeds his instinct as a great sire that he does not even know where he is or that she awaits him — despite her perfume that fills his head to bursting. He is so blind to everything except his urgency that he cannot even recognize her for whom he yearns, her through whom he will at last discharge the genealogical dictates of no less an ancestor than the Godolphin Barb. Yes my dears, this very stallion, this carrier of the precious seed, he too is one of the distant sons of the Godolphin Barb.

"But he sees her! Now! She has appeared to him, she allays his pain. And he changes. Oh, my dears, he changes. Watch what he does. Look there!"

The Old Gentleman ceased talking. He held out both hands for quiet. And suddenly, and as if he too had heard what the Old Gentleman had said, the stallion that had been so fiercely struggling grew calm, became even timorous, and gently approached the brood mare. The blind and maddened look faded from the stallion's eye, the heaving of his chest sub-

Burning Deck Fiction

- **Tom Ahern: THE CAPTURE OF TRIESTE.** The first book of stories by the acclaimed author of *Hecatombs of Lake*. "Seeds of fine satire" - *NY Times Book Review*. 66pp., signed cloth $15, paper $4.
- -:**SUPERBOUNCE.** Short-short stories. 28pp., wrappers $3

- **Jaimy Gordon: CIRCUMSPECTIONS FROM AN EQUESTRIAN STATUE.** A novella about General Burnside, more famous for his "sideburns" than for winning battles. 76pp., signed cloth $15, paper $4

- **John Hawkes: INNOCENCE IN EXTREMIS.** An offshoot from the author's latest novel, *Adventures in the Alaskan Skin Trade*. 100pp., cloth $17.50, paper, sewn $8

- **Lissa McLaughlin: SEEING THE MULTITUDES DELAYED.** An unusual sense of cadence gives these stories on Anna Karenina, Crusoe, salesmen and waiters their immediacy. 76pp., signed cloth $15, paper $4

- **Harry Mathews: COUNTRY COOKING & OTHER STORIES.** As intricate as Mathews' novels, as full of curious learning and devastating satire. 88pp., signed cloth $15, paper $4

- **Gail Sher: BROKE AIDE.** Prose in which "time and location are as elusive as the site of an atom, (but) the subject exists infinitely" - Beverly Dahlen. 80pp., signed cloth $15, paper, sewn $7

- **Dallas Wiebe: THE TRANSPARENT EYE-BALL.** 4 stories by a winner of the Aga Khan Prize. *Library Journal's* selection for 1982. 120pp., paper $4

Please order from:

- Small Press Distribution, 1784 Shattuck Ave., Berkeley, CA 94709
  Inland, PO Box 261, East Haven, CT 06512
  Bookslinger, 213 East 4th St., St. Paul, MN 55101

sided. His groom allowed the lead-rein to go slack. And in the silence the stallion came close to the brood mare where she still stood for him in all her patience, and nudged her, stepped to her other side and rested his gallant head against her neck. He whinnied. He nipped her on the chest, on the neck, on the other side of the neck, then gently shoved her head with his. She stirred. He pressed his wet shoulder to her placid shoulder. He licked her neck. He turned his dark eyes upon her and whinnied.

"There!" whispered the Old Gentleman. "There we have it. The thunder of his blood is stilled — for her, for her. The stallion who cannot help the viciousness of his desire is all at once as tender as you see him now. He means both to arouse and appease the helpless creature whom in another moment he must assault. Even this great stallion, bred and born to the violence of breeding, is capable of pausing in his brute urges for the sake of his mare. The stallion is affectionate, my dears, affectionate! We honor the stallion as we do the mare!

"But wait!" cried the Old Gentleman in tones of elation as well as warning. "He mounts! He mounts! Stand back! Alert yourselves! The stallion mounts!"

Again the abrupt transformation. Again the stallion appeared to have heard and understood what the Old Gentleman had said and now behaved accordingly. Slowly, gradually, the frantic groom maneuvered his explosive charge around the brood

mare, to the rear of her, and into position. Up
clamored the stallion, and slipped off. Up again and
down again ungainly, undaunted, clownish and
princely too in his frothing and fumbling efforts to
mount the mare. The groom pushed him on one side,
the Old Gentleman on the other; in silence the
privileged audience urged him on. His sharp black
hooves churned up the soft earth behind the mare;
his every move gave vent to ruthless determination.
Then up he went. And stayed. He stayed. And again
the sighs of the privileged audience were audible in
the arena's silence, while the Old Gentleman and
the frantic groom exchanged glances and indulged in
a moment's respite and the stallion, half-upended on
the mare like a ship on a rock, held himself aloft in
terror, his wild eyes turned upwards and fixed on
the portrait of an aged stallion depicted elegantly at
rest in a field. He was Harpagon, the brood mare's
sire whose breeding days were done forever.

Uncle Jake squirmed in his chair. He knew without
looking that there was still not a flicker of change in
the disinterested attention with which the young
equestrienne watched the shameful antics of the stallion. For all the trumpeting, and for all the Old
Gentleman's speeches, had she really had eyes for
anything except for the black disfigurement which,
from the first, had made his grandfather's stallion not
a handsome thoroughbred but a freak? Now the
helpless horse was thwarted, as all could see; now his

black disfigurement was like some quite separate
creature to be trapped and tamed. It swelled, it
swayed, it loomed as large as the very horse from
which it hung. What must she think?

"My dears," said the Old Gentleman softly, wryly,
and wiping his face and hands on a silk handkerchief,
"even the act of grace itself may be delayed by distraction, the time of day, a hundred minor matters.
They are no better than ourselves, these stately
animals. But what would they do without us, my
dears. How would they manage?"

So saying the Old Gentleman carressed the stallion's flank with one hand and then stooped and in
the other seized the proud flesh. For an instant he
held it, signet ring gleaming from the second finger
of the steadying hand, and then slipped it home.

"Done!" he cried, wheeling upon his audience and
wiping the instrumental hand on the handkerchief.
"My dears, it is done!"

The stallion heaved.

The brood mare stood her ground.

"My dears," whispered the Old Gentleman as he
watched the red curtains closing after the disappear-
ing brood mare and her stallion, "he does not know
what has happened to him. He does not know what
he has done. But she does, my dears, she does. And
so do we."

Now the Old Gentleman, as drained and listless
as the stallion who had served his function and was

gone, stood alone in the center of the oval arena. And was the clapping for the stallion, the brood mare, or the Old Gentleman? No one could know though it was the old patrician who accepted their applause and bowed and then stood staring from one to the other of his portraits of dead horses as the ovation swelled.

In the ebb and flow of the applause, suddenly and clearly Uncle Jake heard the voice of the young equestrienne. She had not moved, nor was she clapping.

"Which do you prefer," she asked in the voice as pure and clear as her person, "the gentleman horse or the lady horse?"

He listened, it was he to whom her question had been addressed. But stammer as he might, he could not answer.

"Well," she said, confiding in him in the midst of the applause, yet speaking coldly, "my preference is for the lady horse. Beyond a doubt."

By the time Uncle Jake had recovered from being jostled by the woman on his right, and had summoned the courage to turn and look his unacknowledged companion full in the face, she was gone.

He too fled the arena.

The Old Gentleman had reached the height of his orchestrative powers. He could do no more. They had listened, they had clapped, the beautiful deed was done. In his love for his horses he had made manifest his love for his guests. But now the last days of the reunion must run their course without him. He urged on his chefs, his singers, his whippers-in. He did his best, knowing all the while that the surprise and harmony he had brought them to would shortly die and that his spirit, his gallantry, his courage, his good will were not enough to protect them from the collapse that was coming. He had done his best and had failed, as he knew he must. But though he relinquished his powers as an impresario to chance and the discontent of the two *grandes dames*, still the last days, even without his guidance, were oddly true to his magnificence and vision, as if random nature could not escape entirely his sway of the past.

The weather worsened, pitting frost against freezing rain and making of the landscape around the Old Gentleman's chateau a terrain of mud as hard as iron. Five days after the brood mare had been bred to the descendant of the Godolphin Barb, the hunt went forth. Conditions were at their worse, the fox was wily, never again would these riders hunt together so disastrous did this day prove. Uncle Jake fell from his pony while at the same time and in a distant field the son of the Old Gentleman's cherished friend, Monsieur Bufont, summoned a recklessness that far exceeded the bravado of Uncle Jake's own father and made a miscalculation. With a last

and spirited cry of 'halloo!' he crashed to the wet
and frozen ground with a broken neck. Word of the
accident spread throughout the hunt. There was
fright, consternation, the uncapping of silver flasks
of brandy. The dogs were collected, the fox escaped.

Uncle Jake, unaware of what had happened, and
humiliated and sorely bruised by his fall, returned
to the chateau on foot, since his mean-tempered pony
had no sooner dumped his young and inattentive rider
than he had made off, ears back and heels flying. The
Old Gentleman and three of his sons had in the
meantime carried the dead man to the Old Gentleman's chateau, where they had deposited him on a
brocaded divan in the first room that had come to
hand, which happened to be the mysterious woman's
own private library decorated in pinks and grays
and greens according to her subtle tastes. It was no
place to leave a corpse. But leave him they did, one
spur tearing a cruel gash in the divan's gold and
green brocade. Then the men set off to inform
Monsieur Bufont of the tragic news. Behind them
they left the mysterious woman herself to keep vigil
with the corpse. The mysterious woman was dis-
pleased to have her library so peremptorily invaded
and her divan soiled, and she saw no reason to
remain in attendance on a man who had been so
foolish as to break his neck. But in his distraction
the Old Gentleman had thought of asking her to
remain behind and keep vigil with the son of his

cherished friend, and she did so, despite her impatience, displeasure, and boredom.

Uncle Jake, still ignorant of how the hunt had been shattered by one man's fall, arrived at the chateau not minutes after the little library had received its shocking burden. Silence, uncanny silence, had once again descended on the chateau. The maids and kitchen help were whispering; the two *grandes dames* had already learned of the cruel death and were furious anew at the Old Gentleman for allowing such a thing to happen. The Irish matriarch had already declared that she would remain not a day longer in a country where grown men broke their necks and were indecorously brought among women and young boys. She would leave Chantilly on the morrow.

For Uncle Jake there was only emptiness and silence and injured pride; there was nothing to do but wander empty corridors and empty rooms, dripping and leaving muddy footprints on marble floors and carpets dating back to the fourteenth century. Then Uncle Jake found himself standing before a closed door covered in green baize. He hesitated, he shrugged, he pushed open the door. He entered the room and found himself face to face with the dead man on the divan. He thought that the man in the red coat might be his father; he felt faint.

The mysterious woman, who was sitting near the dead man, understood at once what Uncle Jake was thinking.

"Oh, why are you looking at that man?" she asked. "That man is dead. He is the son of your grandfather's cherished neighbor, Monsieur Bufont. He has a broken neck, that man. Your grandfather is sad. He himself is taking the news to Monsieur Bufont.

"But come here," she said, "come sit with me. You may keep me company until they take that man back to his father's chateau where he belongs. The day is ruined, thanks to him. He should have been more careful."

The mysterious woman pointed to the empty ornate chair near hers; Uncle Jake sat down in it.

"Well," she said, "you may remove your cap."

He did so.

"And you? You too are muddy. You too have fallen off your little horse today. Oh, they have all fallen off today. Your grandfather was quite amused until that man killed himself and spoiled everything for the rest of us. But I was not amused. It gives me no pleasure to watch grown men toppling off that way. It's not good for the horses though your grandfather seems not to care. I care. I do not like to see horses running loose and injuring themselves. I do not approve. I do not always share your grandfather's good humor. Well, his humor is not so good today. Monsieur Bufont the elder will not take it well."

She paused. Uncle Jake knew that she was watching him with cocked head like a bird. She was tap-

ping the handle of her whip against a small and
shapely calf buried inside her damp skirts. He kept
his eyes down and clutched his hands. His hunting
cap sat in his lap like a black skull. He wanted to
look over his shoulder and toward the divan but did
not; he wanted to look at the mysterious woman but
could not.

"This room," she said suddenly. "Do you like this
room? It is mine. It is my library. Your grandfather
gave me this room and caused the men to prepare it
according to my tastes. Do you like it? I have my
books, my love seat, my writing desk. No one else
comes here but me. Not even your grandfather. I
cannot think why he took it into his head to leave
that dead man here, in a lady's private library. I am
not happy about this matter. Not at all happy. And
then your grandfather asked me to stay with him.
To attend the corpse. What need is there for that?
As if Monsieur Bufont could appreciate a little *tete-
a-tete* in my library. That man, with his broken neck."

She paused. Her wet skirts rustled. Her breathing
sounded like water moving beneath a crust of ice.

"But you," she continued. "For weeks I have
thought that I should enjoy a little *tete-a-tete* with
you. Are you pleased? I do not invite everyone to
sit with me in such seclusion. Not at all. I would
not allow your brothers to seat themselves beside me
— not for a minute. Do you understand? Not every-
body fathered by a Deauville becomes a Deauville

despite your grandfather's faith in his blood. Your
brothers are of Irish blood, not French. As for that
baby, anyone can see that he should have been left
at home. He pleases no one, that baby. He also is
not a Deauville. But you," she said and paused,
softened her voice, leaned herself slightly in his
direction, "you have the Deauville bones, the Deauville face, the ears. Do you think I don't know? I am
partial to Deauvilles, I recognize no man who has
not the bearing. I am the best judge as your grandfather is the first to say. I cannot be fooled. If I
showed you a portrait of your grandfather as a boy
you would see yourself. And I may tell you this:
I have spoken about you to your grandfather. You
are his favorite. You are my favorite too. Are you
pleased?"

He was chilled, he was fevered, and not for an
instant did the sound of her voice obliterate the
presence of the bulky figure behind his back. And
how could she dismiss Granny and poor Doc the way
she did? And how speak of poor Billy Boy with such
cruel disdain? She assaulted his loyalty with every
compliment she paid him; she drew him to her, she
pushed him away. And could he believe her? Was
he himself so admirable if Granny and Doc were
not? How could he possibly defend himself from her
closeness, her contradictions, her voice like crystals
tinkling?

"Look at me," she said then and he did so. "What is the matter? You must not be uncomfortable with your grandfather's friend. What would he think? You are quite old enough to smile back at me when I smile. Your grandfather smiles handsomely at me and your father too. You must do the same. You must not flinch before the attentions of a lady. But what a pair we are. At least I did not fall off like you though my skirts are muddy."

She laughed. She expected him to laugh as well though he could not. At last he was now able to meet her eyes and to see in her small dark eyes the invitation he did not understand but wished to accept. He stared at the hard surface of her small face; he thought of pearls. Then, making clear that she knew what he was thinking, slowly she removed one of her black gloves and reached out her hand, while holding him with her quick eyes as if daring him to flinch or blush, and brushed back his wet hair and stroked the curve of his ear. The fingers that should have been cold were warm. Again she brushed away his hair, stroked his ear.

"Handsome boy," she said. "What a handsome boy."

He held still. He waited. He knew what it would be like to touch her damp and pearly skin.

"And for that," she said, "I am going to give you a gift. Do you want my gift?"

He nodded.

"Well then, I shall give you something to take home. Something you shall remember. Always. Oh yes," she said, allowing her fingertips to rest on his long and youthful jaw, "you are going home. You did not know? Then I must tell you: your mother has heard what she calls the dreadful news. I do not see why the news is dreadful except to Monsieur Bufont the elder. But she is calling for the trunks already. A man has been killed, she says, and she will not remain. Why not, I should like to ask. How does this dead man concern your mother? She was not nearby when he fell. She did not go to his aid. She was not even in her silly carriage with your grandfather's wife. But now she insists: you are going home. Tomorrow. Not a day later. She is quite insulting to your grandfather, that mother of yours. Does she not know that she has one son who is a Deauville? Is she not proud? Oh no, she loses her temper. She thinks a dead man is the worst thing in the world. So it is tomorrow. Tomorrow.

"Well, I shall not keep you in suspense any longer. You may have your gift."

She sat straight, as if on her horse, and leaned still closer to him and raised her arms, reached behind her neck, and with pretty gestures unfastened the chaste white stock that bound her throat. He watched, he smelled her scent, he knew that he was offending his mother as never before though she was not there.

"You need not look at me that way. It is only a stuffy piece of white cloth. It is mine to remove. You need not worry. Your grandfather says that my throat is like a vase for a flower. But you may look at it. Who will know? And do you see this chain, which is as thin and golden as a hair from the head of a child? Your gift is dangling from the end of this golden chain. Will you draw it forth?"

She reached for his hand and guided his fingers to the almost invisible chain around her throat. Together, her hand on his, they managed to fish to the surface the gift, which was a small gold pendant in the shape of a tear. It was still warm from where it had lain inside her clothing. He could not believe that his own fingers had grazed her throat and, worse or better, had grazed still more of what the removal of the stock had exposed to view: a small bare portion of the upper chest, a brief circlet of the collarbone like a diadem beneath the white skin. In silence, heads together, they studied the golden tear that lay now in his palm, not in hers.

"Your grandfather gave me this locket," she said, her face so close to his that he felt the breath of her words against his cheek. "It is perhaps not quite as beautiful as my rings, which he also gave me, but I am so fond of this little tear that I never remove it from my person. Never. Your grandfather says that it is the dove between my saints. What wickedness! But now I must tell you something about a lady's locket. When a gentleman gives a lady a locket it is understood that no one else shall ever see what hides in the locket. The gentleman and the lady may look inside the locket together. The lady often looks inside it alone. But no one else. No one. The secret of the locket is preserved as carefully as the privacy of the lady in her chamber.

"Now," she whispered, "now you are going to see inside my locket!"

She picked it up from his palm. She opened it. He bent his head.

"Is it nice? Do you like it? Do you know who she is? Do you recognize this young lady's face? Do you? Well, it is mine. That face is mine. I was that girl. Your grandfather posed me in the garden for this portrait. He himself undraped me. He said that he wished the painter could have done his work blindfolded! But I was happy enough to see that painter's eyes on me. Why not? Now do you recognize the resemblance? How clever he was to paint my face, my throat, my shoulders, my upper body on that oval background of purest white. My features and coloration are strongest against the white. Was I not young? Was I not delicious? Now do you understand your grandfather's wickedness? You will. You will.

"Now you have a gift to take home with you!"

She smiled. She closed the locket. He reached for it. Then to his surprise she drew back, raised her brows, let the locket drop once more inside her clothes.

"What? The locket itself? Would I give you my golden tear to put into your trouser pocket? Give you what I have kept on my person all these years? Not at all. Hardly. My gift to you is what is now lodged in your head. The locket is mine. What you have seen is yours. That's enough. Not many boys your age are half so fortunate."

Just then the Old Gentleman and three of his sons, including his ninth, burst grimly upon Uncle Jake and the mysterious woman, and while the Old Gentleman held his face in his hands and wept, his three sons took up the corpse and struggled with it to the waiting carriage. The Old Gentleman took no notice of his grandson, white of face and forlorn, or of she who had kept the vigil.

They caught the dead man's horse which had broken its leg in the accident and shot it. The rain came down and turned to ice. The dogs howled in the kennels.

The next day, true to her word, the Irish matriarch ordered that the trunks and valises and hat boxes be packed. Empty and half-filled pieces of luggage accumulated in the rooms of her charges, blocked the corridors. By mid-afternoon they were ready. At the last moment the two French maids fell to their knees before their French-American master and told him, ruefully, that they were loyal, that

they loved Madame and the young messieurs, but
that having once returned to France they could not
go back. They could not go back to America and
Deauville Farms. Would he allow them to stay?
Would he forgive them? The Old Gentleman watched
his son and grew still darker of visage at this last
vexation, and then, sternly, he singled out two of
his own youngest maids to take the place of the
defaulters.

They donned their wraps. It was snowing and the
first week of November. The mysterious woman and
the Old Gentleman's wife stood side by side to
watch them go. The Irish matriarch led the way to
the carriages. Then she herself descended, walked
back quickly to the Old Gentleman, who was stooped
and scowling in the wreckage of his high hopes,
and flung herself into his grudging arms and kissed
him.

Their return crossing was the worst Atlantic
crossing in nineteen years.

This book was printed by AWEDE in Windsor, Vt. The cover photograph by Ruby Ray was printed in Barre, Vt. at The Northlight Studio Press. The text was linotyped by Mollohan Typesetting in Greenwich, R.I. Smyth-sewn by New Hampshire Bindery in Concord. There are 2500 copies, of which 500 are cloth-bound.